FREE THROW
FAIL

BY JAKE MADDOX

text by
Tyler Omoth

STONE ARCH BOOKS
a capstone imprint

Jake Maddox JV books are published by Stone Arch Books
A Capstone Imprint
1710 Roe Crest Drive
North Mankato, Minnesota 56003
www.mycapstone.com

Library of Congress Cataloging-in-Publication Data is available on the Library of Congress website.

ISBN: 978-1-4965-4941-9 (library binding)
ISBN: 978-1-4965-4943-3 (paperback)
ISBN: 978-1-4965-4945-7 (eBook PDF)

Editor: Nate LeBoutillier
Art Director: Russel Greismer
Designer: Kayla Rossow
Media Researcher: Eric Gohl
Production Specialist: Tori Abraham

Photo Credits:
Shutterstock: cristovao, cover, Lane V. Erickson, 4, 12, 40, 48, 58, Oleg Mikhaylov, cover (background), Vasilyev Alexandr, back cover, chapter openers (background)

Printed and bound in Canada.
010392F17

TABLE OF CONTENTS

CHAPTER 1

HOWLING AT THE MOON

Coach Davis stood at the front of the team bus. He wore a sweatshirt that read "Tyndall Tigers" across the front. As he faced the rear of the bus, his hands gripped seats on each side of the aisle. "Let me hear it, everybody," he said. "Who's going to win tonight?"

"Tigers! Tigers! Tigers!" the team shouted.

The bus shook as the players pumped their fists in the air with each exclamation.

"That's what I like to hear," Coach Davis said. He sat down in the driver's seat and turned the key. "Sounds like victory."

Every road game started the same way. Coach Davis asked them who would win, they yelled out *Tigers!*, and then the bus would rumble away from Tyndall Junior High.

As the bus hit the highway and headed toward the next opponent's town, the Tigers' point guard, Mike, spoke up. "Guys," Mike said, "it's been a good season so far. But I think we're missing something that all the great teams have."

Teammates looked at one another and shrugged. They looked back at Mike.

"Like what?" said Chuck, the power forward. "We have steady ball handling, great shooters, solid defense, and tough rebounders. What more do we need?"

"Nicknames," Mike said. He waggled his eyebrows. "Think about it. King James, Durantula, The Splash Brothers. Even guys from the old days, like Air Jordan. All the great players out there have nicknames."

The guys on the team started to laugh and turn back to their previous conversations. But Mike wasn't going to let it go that easily.

"Hey, I'm serious," said Mike. "I've given this some thought. I think I should be *The Wizard*."

"Why is that?" said Reggie. "Because your smelly shoes make everyone disappear?"

"No, because I find the open man and dish out assists like magic!" Mike said.

Groans arose from the guys. Someone threw a candy wrapper at Mike.

Mike ducked and popped back up. "So who's next?" he said.

"I'll go," said Reggie. "I'm the tallest guy and the center, but I'm also the best jumper. I win tip-offs and rip down rebounds, so I think you guys should call me *Hops*."

"That's lame, but fine," said Chuck. "My turn." He stood up in the aisle. He wasn't as tall as Reggie, but what he lacked in height, he made up for in brawn. He flexed his biceps and twisted his face into a snarl.

Someone nearly spit his Gatorade.

"Fear me!" Chuck said. "I box out with power. I set picks that knock players on their tails. I rumble through the lane like a bear with a bad attitude. I am *The Grizzly*. But you can just call me *Grizz*."

When the laughs died down, Mike said, "What about you, Leo?"

Leo ran his fingers through his dark shoulder-length hair. "Just call me *Lockdown*," he said.

Chuck's face contorted into a confused grimace. "Lockdown?" he said "What kind of nickname is that? Are you a prison guard?"

"No," Mike said. "He's our best defender. He takes the other team's best shooter and locks him down. I like it."

"How about you, Jake?" Mike said.

From the very back seat of the bus, Jake grinned and shrugged. He was a shy guy and had never had a nickname. "I don't know," he said. "I'm good with Jake."

"What? No," said Mike. "You're our best scorer. When I flip you the ball, you let it fly from anywhere."

"And it usually goes in," said Preston, one of the bench players.

"You have the sweetest jumper in the conference," said Mike.

"How about *Sweety J*?" said Chuck. "You know, J for Jake and J for Jumper."

"Isn't that what you nicknamed your last girlfriend, Chuck?" someone said.

"That girl was never Chuck's girlfriend," said Mike. "She turned him down for the Autumn Dance."

"Hey, that's mean," said Chuck. He sighed. "But unfortunately, true."

"*Jump Shot Jake*," Reggie said.

Jake smiled.

"Yeah," Leo said, "that's cool. Or we could just call him *JJ*."

"Now we're talking," Mike said.

A few familiar guitar chords came through the bus's stereo speakers.

"Hey, Coach, turn it up!" Chuck said. "It's Hunter Moon!"

Coach Davis gave a small nod in the mirror. He reached over to crank the dial on the radio. Guys began playing air guitar and drums.

Coach Davis tuned the radio to KTYN, the local country music station, on the way to every road game. Though most of the guys listened to other stuff normally, many of them listened to country radio happily, just for the chance to hear Hunter Moon.

Hunter Moon was an interesting character. He had grown up playing in a polka band with his family from the age of four before switching over to country music and hitting it big. Legend had it that he had also been a ballplayer, himself. A good one.

The guys knew a lot about Hunter Moon because he also happened to be from Tyndall. He had actually played for Coach Davis and the Tyndall Tigers when he was a middle schooler.

The whole team whooped and sang along with Hunter Moon's latest hit song, "Blowin' Off Steam." As the team bus rocked its way toward their next opponent, Jake laughed. He wasn't too shy to howl along with the rest of them.

CHAPTER 2

FOUL TROUBLE

The referee looked at Reggie and then at the Bearcats' starting center. He gave a quick nod, blew his whistle, and tossed the basketball straight up into the air. Both players leapt, but Reggie's outstretched hand was at least a foot higher than his opponent's. He tipped the ball back to Mike.

Mike caught the ball and dribbled through the defense. As he raced towards the hoop, one defender beat him to the basket, waiting to block his shot.

Mike hit the brakes, spun to his right, and flipped the ball to the corner.

Jake was there waiting. He had set his feet so that when the ball reached him, he was in perfect shooting position. He caught the ball, jumped, and let it fly.

Swish! The score was already 3-0 in favor of the Tigers.

The game rolled on just like the Tigers hoped it would. Mike really looked like a wizard. He played great defense and kept the ball away from defenders. He dished out passes to open teammates. In the second quarter, he even lobbed one from half court all the way toward the basket for Reggie. Reggie launched himself upward, caught the ball, and laid it in. It was a perfect alley-oop.

Jake's shot was on. He hit pull-up jumpers and wide-open 3-pointers throughout the first half. When the buzzer sounded to end the first half, the

Tigers were ahead, 34-18. The team hit the locker room for the short halftime.

"Listen up," Coach Davis said. "That was a great start, but we can't rest easy. Jake, keep knocking down those shots. Reggie, good job on the boards, but don't bring the ball down to your waist when you grab an offensive board. Keep it up high and go right back up for the shot. Leo, keep your feet on D. Don't bite on the fake when your guy pumps. Mike, keep finding the open guy. And we need more energy from our bench. Whether you're on the floor or not, I want everybody into it."

Coach Davis grabbed a nearby water bottle and took two big chugs. He was sweating nearly as much as the players.

"Hey!" said Chuck, "What about me?"

Coach Davis cracked a smile. "You just keep on being a bear. They don't know how to handle you, *Grizz*."

They all laughed as Chuck put on a cocky smile. They'd never suspected that Coach Davis was listening to them on the bus.

The second half's opening possession went just like the first one. Mike got the ball and charged for the basket. Once again cut off, he stopped, spun, and flipped the ball to Jake. On the wing, Jake caught the ball and jumped up, ready to shoot. Before he could release the shot, an opposing player flew at Jake, hacking him on the wrist.

Tweet!

The referee called a foul on the play.

Jake stepped up to the free throw line as the two teams lined up for the shot. He wiped his hands on his shorts, but they still felt clammy to him. He took a deep breath as the ref tossed him the ball.

No sweat. Jake thought to himself. That's what his mom always used to say about free throws: "No sweat! They're easy."

Jake wiped his hands on his shorts again. He was sweating plenty now.

"You've got this, Jake," Mike said.

Jake wasn't so sure. He felt like every eye in the gym was on him. He imagined that he could feel a small spot, the size of a quarter, on his back burning where Coach Davis's eyes were focused.

Images of countless practices at home with his own hoop ran through his mind. He could actually hear the instructions in his mother's voice. She'd played college hoops when she was younger and coached him at home for hours each week.

Take a breath. Relax. Set your pattern. Visualize the ball going through the hoop. Elbow in, and let it go.

Jake dribbled the ball two times. He paused just long enough to imagine it going through the basket. He shot the ball.

With a clank, the ball bounced off the front of the rim.

Jake swore he heard someone groan. He looked at Chuck, who shot him a dark glare. The ref got the ball back and then tossed it to Jake for a second shot.

Jake visualized practicing again.

This time his mom wasn't there. It was just him and the hoop. Suddenly, his father came outside to where he was standing at the free throw line. On his face was a dazed expression. There was a phone in his hand.

"There's been a car accident," he said. "Mom's gone."

The images of this moment flickered in Jake's mind. Jake looked up at the hoop. It began to blur slightly.

That was two years ago, he thought to himself. *Let it go.*

He dribbled two times, launched the ball, and watched it smack the backboard and bounce away yet again. Luckily for the Tigers, Reggie jumped up and grabbed the rebound, putting it back in for two.

The rest of the game went much like the first half with one major exception. The opposing team fouled Jake anytime he shot the ball, if they could. Jake still managed to get up a few shots and even scored six more points. But he'd also missed 13 free throws — and made none.

When the final horn sounded, the Tigers had won again, but it had been close. Other players had to step up their usual game to cover for points they were used to getting from Jake.

Coach Davis walked into the locker room and faced them. "That was one heck of a game, guys," he said. "Many of you did what you needed to do to get the W. Mike even had 16 points. That's a career high for him."

Mike smiled, but not big. The guys knew that there was a message underneath Coach Davis's compliment.

"All right," said Coach Davis. "Let's get home, now, and get some rest."

Despite the victory, the bus ride home was quiet except for the sound of the bus tires on the pavement. Finally, Chuck spun around in his seat and broke the silence.

"JJ, you have the sweetest shot I've ever seen. You drain runners and fadeways and pull-up 3-pointers with defenders in your face. So how is it that you can't hit *any* free throws?"

Jake didn't say anything. He kept staring out the bus window, wishing he was already home.

CHAPTER 3

PRACTICE PRESSURE

Coach Davis blasted his whistle, and the Tigers all groaned. "Everybody on the line," Coach Davis said. "Tiger Prowl."

The guys hated the Tiger Prowl drill, but they knew that physical conditioning was a key to their success. They stood on the baseline, ready to run. When Coach Davis blew his whistle again, they ran to the closest free throw line and back. Then they ran to the half court line and back. Then the opposite free throw line and back. Then all the way down to the far baseline and back.

Each time they reached a line they had to touch their hands to the line on the floor. It was a drill of back-and-forth sprints that made them dig deep and improve their conditioning. They needed to find the strength to keep going.

Today, they were lucky. They did only two Tiger Prowls.

"Okay, that's enough. Huddle up," Coach Davis said. "You guys really came together as a team and picked each other up last game. However, it also highlighted some weaknesses."

Chuck snorted and then took two fake dribbles and a deep breath. Then he shot a fake free throw and said, "Clank!"

"Knock it off, Grizz," Coach Davis said. "Obviously, we had some free throw issues, but that's not all. Our bigs are getting boards, but they need more help from the rest of you. Everyone needs to rebound. Also, we had 19 turnovers. That's way too many."

For the rest of practice, they did drills to strengthen the weakest parts of their game. They worked on boxing out, making smart passes, and handling the ball. Each time they thought they were done, Coach Davis made them run the drill a few more times.

It was an exhausting but productive practice. When Coach blew the whistle that ended it all, they were grateful.

As they started to leave the gym, Coach Davis spoke up. "Jake," he said. "I need you to stay just a little longer."

Jake cringed. He could hear Chuck chortling as the rest of the team walked away.

"What's up, Coach?" Jake said.

"Let's see if we can get to the bottom of your free throw issue," Coach Davis said. "Shoot a hundred. I'll rebound."

Jake stepped up to the line, looking briefly over his shoulder at the last of his teammates heading off to the locker room. Coach Davis tossed him the ball, and he caught it cleanly. Jake went through his usual free throw routine. Two dribbles, a deep breath, visualize, and let it go.

Swish!

Coach Davis grabbed the ball and flipped it back to him. "That's one," he said. "You made that look really easy. Let's do that ninety-nine more times."

One after another, Jake shot free throws, and Coach Davis returned the ball to him. He didn't make them all, but he made most of them. After he shot his 40th free throw, another clean make, he was 33 for 40.

This time Coach Davis didn't throw the ball back to him, but tucked it under his own arm.

"Thirty-three for forty," he said. "That's better than eighty percent. That's not just okay shooting, that's great shooting. Why can't you do it in the game?"

"I dunno," Jake said. "It's just practice, I guess. If I miss one, it doesn't really matter."

Coach Davis tossed the ball back to Jake. "Okay," he said. "I get that."

Jake dribbled and shot.

Swish.

"Where'd you learn to shoot like this anyway?" asked Coach Davis, grabbing the ball and tossing it to Jake.

Jake caught the ball again. "My mom used to play college ball." He took another shot.

Clank.

"Ah," Coach Davis said. "I see. Shoot a couple more, now."

Jake shot twice more but missed each one.

Coach Davis jogged over to retrieve the ball. "Were you thinking about the other guys watching you just now?" Coach Davis asked.

"Yeah, kind of," Jake said. He wiped his hands on his shorts.

"Quick shot!" said Coach Davis, throwing a hard chest pass to Jake.

Without even thinking, Jake caught the pass, spun, and put up a high-arcing shot. It was perfect.

"See that?" said Coach Davis. "You're a natural, kid. You may be thinking a little too much out there when everything is stopped, and you're on the line."

Jake wiped his hands on his shorts.

"Don't worry about it, Jake," Coach Davis said. "I'm not worried about you. You're going to be fine. Go on. Get out of here."

"Thanks, Coach," Jake said.

CHAPTER 4

FLAGRANT FAIL

The Tigers huddled by their bench as they prepared to take the court against the Crofton Cardinals. A big crowd showed up for the game, and it was hard to hear over the noise. It didn't matter. They knew what Coach Davis was going to say.

"Another team, another win," Coach Davis said. "Who's going to win tonight?"

"Tigers! Tigers! Tigers!" they shouted in unison.

They all high-fived each other and ran out to midcourt for the tip off for their next game.

Reggie took his normal spot in the jump ball circle with Mike behind him. Each player jockeyed for the best position. As Jake moved to get in front of an opposing player, he felt an elbow dig into his ribs. He glanced sideways.

His opponent, number thirty-four, was a beast. His shoulders were twice as wide as Jake's, and his hands were the size of dinner plates.

Number thirty-four sneered at Jake. "Hey, twenty-two," he said. "I looked up your stats online from last game. If I were you, I'd get ready to start shooting some free throws."

The player laughed and stepped on one of Jake's feet as the jump ball went up. Reggie tipped the ball to Mike. Mike spun around to find Jake for the opening jumper but couldn't find him.

Jake was still at half court. The Beast's foot stomp had tripped him up.

Mike dribbled out from the basket and then threw it in to Reggie in the post. Reggie faked to his right, spun around to his left, and put up a bank shot that went in for two.

"Where were you?" Mike asked as they ran back on defense.

Jake said, "Next time I'll be there."

Before the other team could get a shot off, Leo jumped the passing lane and stole the ball. He threw it to Mike, who charged down the court. When Mike saw Jake angling in from the right wing, he fired a bounce pass to him. Jake caught the pass behind the 3-point line and stopped cold. He jumped up to shoot. As Jake released the ball, The Beast ran by and smacked Jake's elbow. The ball flew wide of its mark.

The ref blew his whistle and signaled for three free shots to come. Jake walked to the foul line. He reminded himself of what Coach Davis had said about thinking too much. Maybe he shouldn't try to worry about all of the visualization and things his mom had taught him.

No pressure.

The referee threw the ball to Jake, and Jake dribbled two times. He could see Chuck already shaking his head out of the corner of his eye. Jake shot the ball, waiting to hear the inevitable clank of a miss.

The shot made no sound until it hit the ground. Jake hadn't just missed — he'd missed *everything*.

Airball!

Jake winced as he heard the taunts and laughs from the crowd. He looked around. Every eye in the gym was on him. Other students, parents, and coaches were looking at him. Even the cheerleaders stood with their pompoms by their sides, giggling. The Beast threw back his head in laughter.

Jake wanted to run. He wanted to skip the rest of the game and just run to the locker room, but he knew that was not possible.

"Time out!" Coach Davis said.

The team plodded over to the bench. Jake was the last one to get there.

"Okay, chin up, Jake," Coach Davis said. "You're fine. You're just thinking too much again. This time, I want you to think about your favorite baseball play from last year."

"Baseball?" Reggie said. "You mean hoops, right Coach?"

"Nope," said Coach Davis. "You played second base, right, Jake? Think about turning a double play or fielding a hot grounder in the hole. Forget everything and just let the ball go. No worries."

"I'll give it a try," Jake said.

The referee blew the whistle, and both teams lined up for the remaining two free throws. The ref threw Jake the ball.

Jake tried to think about baseball. In game two of a double-header against Caledonia last season, he had three hits. Though none of them were home runs or even great hits, they kept getting through.

That was a good day on the diamond.

He took his two dribbles and shot the ball. The basketball hit the front of the rim, bounced off the backboard, and settled into the net.

He'd made it.

He got the ball for his third shot and tried to repeat the process, but now he was thinking about basketball again. No matter how hard he tried to think about the three-hit baseball game, his eyes brought him back to the gymnasium. Jake dribbled and fired.

Clank!

The rest of the game went on just like that. Coach Davis tried to set up double screens to get Jake open for quick-hitting shots. But the Cardinals continued to foul Jake. Though three of their players had already fouled out, the strategy was working. With only four minutes left in the game, the Cardinals led the Tigers by six points. Jake had made only one of sixteen free throws.

Mike dribbled down the court. He faked a pass to Leo on the left side but then turned and fired it to Jake. Jake grabbed the pass and dribbled to the right, looking for an open spot. He jumped up to shoot, and The Beast plowed into him. The next thing Jake knew, he was on the floor. And his shoulder hurt.

The ref signaled to a Cardinal player and said, "Flagrant foul on number thirty-four."

The Beast sneered. He smiled at Jake. "Try not to break the rim, Hot Shot," he said.

Jake jumped up and ran over to The Beast. Without thinking, he shoved him so hard that The Beast fell over backward.

The gym fell silent. Everything seemed frozen in time.

Then the referee's whistle blew again with a piercing screech. "Technical foul, number twenty-two," said the ref to the scorer's table. To Jake he said, "You'd better cool it, kid."

Jake pointed at The Beast. "Why don't you tell this guy to cool it?" said Jake to the ref. "They've been smacking me around all game!"

The referee blew his whistle again and signaled another technical foul. "That's it, kid," he said. "You're out of the game."

Before Jake could respond, Chuck grabbed Jake and led him to the bench.

Jake didn't even care. He headed for the very end of the bench. He didn't want to talk to anyone at all.

"Not so fast, Tough Guy," Coach Davis said. "You're going to be sitting right next to me."

Jake took his seat next to the coach and covered his head with a towel. He couldn't watch as the team finished the game without him. The Tigers lost, 48-44.

CHAPTER 5

LONGEST BUS RIDE

When the team got on the bus, Jake flopped down in the fourth seat from the front instead of way in the back where he usually sat. He wasn't close to the coaches or his teammates, and that's just how he wanted it.

The rest of the team and Coach Davis filed onto the bus. The air was heavy with frustration. Even Coach Davis looked like he'd run out of good things to say. No one said a word as the bus pulled away and bounced toward home. Thankfully, Coach Davis turned on the radio to KTYN.

Jake stared out at the brown autumn landscape. Fields of chopped corn stalks streaked by the window. It was that time of year when fall colors had passed, crops were harvested, and the view was a mixture of browns and grays. The glass of the window was cold against Jake's forehead.

He thought about the game. He couldn't forget the sound of the crowd yelling *Airball!* He could still feel the constant hacks and slaps on his hands and arms as he tried to shoot. He rubbed his shoulder where a bruise would soon surely form.

The bus rolled on for 20 minutes in silence. The only sound was the radio, but Jake wasn't listening, even when a Hunter Moon song came on. Thankfully, it was a slow, sad one. He wished he was in one of those science fiction movies where they could just teleport him home, right into his room. That way, he wouldn't even have to talk to his dad.

After half an hour, the silence was stifling.

At least that's how Chuck must've felt when he finally spoke up. He stood up from his seat in the back of the bus and threw his arms out at Jake.

"What is wrong with you?" Chuck said.

Jake didn't even turn his head.

"How is it even possible?" Chuck said. "I mean, you can hit jumpers from all over, but you can't hit a stinking free throw. Do you know why they call it a free throw? Because it's free. It's a gimme!"

Jake looked around the bus. Leo and Reggie were pretending to look at their phones. Everyone else was either staring out a window or staring straight ahead.

"I think we should take back your nickname," Chuck said. "You're not Jump Shot Jake any more. You're the Foul Shot Failure."

Jake turned slowly, not to look at Chuck but at Mike. Mike met Jake's gaze and shrugged. Silently, he mouthed *ignore him* as he nodded his head towards Chuck.

"I don't know, man," Chuck said, "I can't see how we can win with Jake on the line all game."

"Okay, that's enough," Coach Davis said. He pulled the bus over.

"Jake had a bad game," Coach Davis said. He looked at Jake, "Sorry, bud, but there's no denying that. You've had better nights. But basketball is a team sport."

Guys continued looking away. It was an awkward moment that no one wanted to deal with.

Coach Davis began to pace the aisle. "Leo," he said, "you missed two layups. Mike, how many turnovers did you have? And none of you were moving your feet on defense or rebounding the way you need to for us to win. We're going to get this figured out, but until then, I don't want to hear any of you offering any criticism of a teammate unless it's constructive criticism."

"But how can we win if our best shooter can't get off a shot without being fouled?" Leo asked.

"Yeah," Chuck said. "With Jake on the line, all we can do is hope for a rebound."

"I said that's enough," said Coach Davis.

The bus was as silent as a graveyard for several seconds. Jake felt like he couldn't even hear any of his teammates breathing.

Just then, the song on the radio stopped and the DJ began to speak. For the next moment, the guys listened as the DJ announced that Tyndall's very own Hunter Moon would be coming back home for a concert at the Tyndall Event Center next Saturday night. Even Coach Davis's eyes went wide.

The guys in the bus wanted to cheer, but it clearly wasn't quite the right moment for that.

CHAPTER 6

REBOUNDING WITH DAD

Jake stood outside his house, trying to spin his basketball on his fingertip. He wasn't very good at it, but it was fun to try. With a deep breath, he looked at the basketball hoop in his driveway.

When his family had set up the hoop five years ago, his mom had insisted right away that they measure out 15 feet to the free throw line. A gray line of duct tape marked the distance. When the duct tape eventually wore away, a painted line took its place.

Jake stepped up to the line, dribbled two times, and shot the ball.

The shot hit the front of the rim, bounced off the backboard, and fell in through the hoop. It wasn't pretty, but it counted.

Jake heard the front door open and close again. He turned around to find his dad leaning on the garage, watching him. His dad was sipping from his usual mug. The mug read *Web Designer Powered by Coffee.*

"How many have you shot?" he asked.

"About fifty," Jake said.

His dad bent to set his coffee mug on the walkway. He walked over and stood underneath the hoop. "How about a few more?" he said. "I'll rebound for you."

"Sure," Jake said.

He walked back to the line to fire up another shot. The ball went in, and his father caught it on the first bounce. He threw the ball back to Jake with a motion that looked more like a shot-put throw than a basketball pass.

"What's your free throw percentage today?" asked his father.

"Maybe seventy or eighty," said Jake.

Jake shot again. This time it was a swish. His dad scooped up the ball and threw it back to him. Jake had to bend over to catch it at his feet.

"Not bad," his dad said. "Right?"

"No, but it doesn't matter," Jake said. "I'm shooting about five percent in actual games. I'm going to end up on the bench if I can't start making my free throws."

Jake shot again, making his third shot in a row. His dad tried to catch it, but missed. The ball bounced off his foot and rolled out into the street. Jake ran out to stop it before it rolled too far.

"Oops," his dad said. "I wish I could offer you some shooting advice. That was always your mom's gift, though. If she were here, she'd know how to fix your shot."

Jake sighed.

He dribbled and then shot. This time, the ball hit hard off the back of the rim and ricocheted high into the air.

"Yeah?" Jake said. "Well, it doesn't matter, does it? She's not here."

Jake's dad chased down the rebound, but Jake could barely see him standing at the edge of the driveway holding the basketball. Jake's vision was suddenly blurred by the tears filling his eyes. Jake turned away from his dad so that he wouldn't see.

"Jake," his dad said.

Jake turned and ran to the front door. He flung it open and ran inside, leaving the door wide open behind him. He bounded up the stairs and locked himself in his room. He flopped down on the bed and punched his pillow twice.

Jake was surprised that it was twenty minutes before he heard a tapping on his bedroom door.

"Hey, Jake," his dad said, "can I talk to you for a bit?"

Jake swallowed the lump in his throat. He sat upright on the bed. "Yeah," he said. He rose and unlocked the door.

His dad opened the door and walked in. He picked up a small basketball that was sitting on the desk and rolled it back and forth in his hands. He sat down next to Jake on the bed. "I'm sorry I haven't been to more games," he said. "I guess I've been too busy trying to earn enough money for us to stay in this house."

"I don't care," Jake said.

"You mean that, Jake?" his dad said. He looked at his son. "Honestly, I don't know if you want me there or not. Basketball was always Mom's thing, and I thought you might resent me trying to take her place."

"Basketball was our thing," Jake said, "but now it's my thing. And it's a pain."

"I have pain, too, Jake," said his dad. "Just the thought of sitting in those bleachers watching you without her is painful for me to deal with. Not to mention a million other things."

Jake looked at his dad, who was wiping his eyes. It hurt Jake to see that. He felt bad that he'd forgotten that his dad was hurting, too.

"It's probably best if we share some of that pain," said Jake's dad. "I've been told that by counselors. But I'm not great at it."

Jake took the ball out of his dad's hands and tried spinning it on his finger. "You used to come to games with her when I was little," he said. "I liked that. You shouldn't have stopped coming."

"I know," said his dad. He snatched the ball from Jake with surprising quickness. He tried spinning it on his own finger but failed.

Jake smiled. "Mom could spin it for a minute straight," he said.

"She could do a lot of things better than me," said Jake's dad. "But that doesn't mean I need to stop trying. When's your next game?"

"We play Seneca tomorrow," Jake said. "It's a home game."

"I'll be there," Jake's dad said. He flipped the ball to his son.

Jake smiled. "Don't start yelling again, though," he said. "You probably won't even know what you're talking about. And we have, you know, enough noisy parents out there."

"Okay," his dad said. "Now, should we get back out there and finish the free throws? You want to be ready for tomorrow night, right?"

Jake led the way back to the hoop in the driveway. For the next half hour, he practiced his free throws while his dad awkwardly rebounded for him. It wasn't like when he'd play with his mom. She'd put him through drills and challenge Jake to games of one-on-one and H-O-R-S-E.

For all that, Jake realized that his dad was making an effort. Every little bit probably helped.

CHAPTER 7

PASSING FANCY

The team huddled by the bench, ready to take on the Seneca Owls. It was an even bigger crowd than last time. Coach Davis kept to tradition.

"Another team, another win," Coach Davis said. "Who's going to win tonight?"

"Tigers! Tigers! Tigers!"

They smacked high-fives and jogged to center court. As the Tigers took their spots for the tip-off, Jake glanced into the stands. His dad sat ten rows up and waved. Jake wiped his hands on his shorts.

Once again, Jake was positioned next to a brute who looked like he could bench-press a tank.

The player scowled at Jake.

That's just fine, Tank, Jake thought. *This time I have a plan.*

As always, Reggie won the tip-off and flipped the ball back to Mike. Mike drove toward the lane, stopped short, and rifled the ball to the corner where Jake was already in position.

Jake caught the ball and saw two Owls players rushing toward him. He knew they had no intention of blocking or disrupting his shot — they were there for the foul. He also knew that one of them was supposed to be guarding Mike. Jake fired a pass right back to Mike, who put up an easy six-foot jumper. The shot rattled home, and the Tigers had a 2-0 lead.

As the Tigers ran down to the other side of the court, Mike ran over to him and said, "Nice pass. Are you going to start taking all of my assists now?"

Jake didn't say anything. He just pointed up at the scoreboard and smiled. Then he sprinted over to cover his man as the Owls brought the ball up the court. It was too late. The Owls' point guard whizzed a football-style pass, and the player Jake was supposed to be guarding made an easy layup.

"Whoa," Chuck said. "These dudes are fast."

Chuck was right. The Owls were the fastest team the Tigers had played yet. But, thanks to Coach Davis's fondness for the Tiger Prowl drill, the Tigers matched them step for step.

Jake put all his effort into his defense. He stayed glued to Tank, shuffling his feet and keeping his hands up. Every time Tank got the ball, Jake was already there with one arm out defending against any quick pass or shot.

On the other end of the court, Jake quickly passed the ball whenever he got it. The Owls players couldn't foul him if he got rid of it quick enough. At first it worked. He found Reggie underneath for a couple of quick assists and even threw a cross-court pass to Leo.

Pretty soon, the Owls players realized that Jake was looking to dish the ball as soon as he got it. They played off him, trying to predict his passes. Mike continued to run the offense.

Just before the half, the Tigers were up 26-22. Coach Davis yelled out the play call, and Mike took charge. He held up his left hand with two fingers up while he dribbled with his right.

The team took their positions and jumped into motion. Jake ran at Leo, stopping to set a pick on Leo's man. As Leo ran around the pick, Mike fired the ball to him. Jake spun off and towards an open spot on the floor. Leo jumped and passed the ball to him.

With ten seconds left on the clock before the half, Jake had the ball, and he was all alone. He heard Coach Davis yell, "Shoot it!" But Jake thought he could sense a defender coming at him. He spun and fired the ball back towards Mike.

His pass never made it.

The Owls' point guard jumped the lane, stealing the ball. He sprinted down the court for a buzzer-beating layup.

The halftime score was 26-24 in favor of the Tigers. Jake had six assists, but zero points. In fact, he hadn't taken a single shot.

In the locker room, Coach Davis didn't look like a coach whose team was winning. He sat down on a bench and looked around the room silently. After a minute or two, Jake noticed that the guys were doing anything they could not to look at their coach. Some were re-tying their shoes while others stared down at their hands. The air felt thick and heavy in the locker room already. The silence made it nearly unbearable.

Finally, Coach Davis spoke.

"What in the world was that?" he said. "Yeah, these guys are fast, but we can handle that." He wiped the sweat from his head with a towel. "You see, we're a team. We're like ants."

Chuck broke the tension by letting loose a chuckle. "Ants?" he said. "We're like ants?"

"Yes, ants!" yelled Coach Davis. "Every ant has a job. You each have a job. If you don't do your job, the ant colony will crumble! Now, get out there and be ants!"

The whole team jumped to their feet and scurried towards the door.

Chuck looked at Reggie. "So if we're ants," he said, "does that mean Coach Davis is the queen ant of the colony?"

"I don't know," Reggie said. "That was weird."

As Jake ran out, he felt a hand grab him by the shoulder.

"Not so fast," Coach Davis said. He spun Jake around. "Sit down."

Jake sat on the bench.

"What's going on?" Coach Davis said. "You're our best scorer, and you haven't put up a single shot yet. This isn't hot potato. This is basketball."

"I have six assists, and my guy only has four points," Jake said. "I'm just trying to help the team, not hurt it."

"What's the score?" Coach Davis asked.

"Twenty-six to twenty-four," Jake said.

"Exactly," Coach Davis said. "When our offense is running right, we usually have a good thirty-five points up on that board by halftime."

"I was thinking that if I really just focus on defense, we could still win," Jake said.

Coach Davis rubbed his face with his hands. "You need to shoot in the game. Now get out there and get a few warm-up shots up," he said. "I'll figure something out."

Jake shuffled out to join his team. He took turns with the other players rebounding and shooting from different spots on the floor. Finally, the buzzer sounded again to end halftime.

At the bench, the players formed a huddle around Coach Davis.

"Let's go get 'em, guys," he said. "Remember what I said. Be ants!"

Then he said something that shocked the whole team. "Cooper, you're in," Coach Davis said. "Jake, grab some pine."

Jake sat on the bench next to Coach Davis. He watched Mike bring the ball up the court and sling it over to Leo. Leo drove the lane but then passed the ball back out to Cooper. He caught the ball and immediately shot it. The ball went in, and the Tigers' lead jumped to four points.

For the rest of the game, the Tigers played better. Cooper couldn't shoot like Jake, but he wasn't too bad, either. He also hit three of his four free throws.

Jake couldn't help but to look back over his shoulder at the home crowd. His eyes found his dad, who was chatting with some stranger with a funny beard next to him. Jake's dad was finally here, and Jake was riding the pine. Perfect.

Jake's dad smiled at him and waved. Jake nodded and turned back to focus on the game.

The Tigers won 56-48, and the locker room echoed with music and laughter again.

Jake wasn't laughing, however. He knew he'd let his team down.

On the ride home, Jake didn't want to talk.

"I had fun watching you play," his dad said. "And it brought back memories. Good memories. You looked a lot like your mother out there."

Jake just stared out the window and tried not to think about the game. As the car pulled into the driveway, Jake recalled seeing his dad sitting with the guy with the beard. "Who were you sitting with tonight?" Jake asked.

"Just an old friend," his dad said.

Jake thought that was weird, but he didn't feel like having a whole conversation about it. He nodded and left it at that.

CHAPTER 8

DAD'S PLAN

The Tigers had a light practice on Friday after the win on Thursday. Since they had a tournament on Saturday, Coach Davis wanted the boys to get some rest. As Jake turned the corner to his block on his walk home, he noticed a strange car parked by the curb outside his house.

As he got closer, he saw his dad was waiting outside, talking with another man. The man looked similar to the guy he sat next to at Jake's last game. But this guy didn't have any fuzzy beard. The stranger spun Jake's basketball on one finger.

Jake paused for a moment to watch the ball whirling around and around. The ball seemed as if it could balance there, spinning, forever.

As Jake reached the end of the driveway, his dad waved to him. He was grinning like Jake hadn't seen him grin in years.

The man turned around. It was definitely the same man from the basketball game, but something was different. He had sunglasses pushed up on top of his head. He wore a T-shirt that read, "Homegrown Tour 2017."

"Hi, Jake," he said.

It was Hunter Moon!

"Umm . . ." Jake said. "Hi. You're Hunter Moon. Why are you in my driveway?"

"Were you wearing a beard for, like, a disguise at my last game?" Jake asked.

Hunter and Jake's dad laughed.

"A music star who would just show up in a gym full of kids would get mobbed," Jake's dad said.

Jake smiled for the first time all day.

"I still have some work to do," his dad said, "so I'll head back in. You two don't need me in the way." His dad turned and walked into the house.

Jake was left standing in the driveway with Hunter Moon.

"Wanna shoot some hoops?" Hunter said.

"Sure," Jake said. He dropped his backpack on the lawn. He didn't know what else to say.

"Your dad tells me you're having a little trouble at the free throw line," Hunter said. He spun around and flipped a shot up. It was a perfect bank shot.

"Yeah," Jake said, "I'm a decent shooter, really. But I just don't like free throws. The other teams have been fouling me every time I get the ball."

"Ah," Hunter said. "They're hacking you. Not cool. Why don't you take to the line, and let's try some right now?"

Jake stepped up to painted foul line in the driveway. Hunter threw him the ball. Jake went through his usual dribbles and deep breaths and tossed up a good shot.

"That looked good," Hunter said. "I don't see any problem there."

"Thanks," Jake said. Hunter threw him the ball again, "Can I ask you something?"

"You bet," Hunter said.

"How do you know my dad?"

"From a long time ago," Hunter said. "We had a mutual connection in your mom."

Jake's next shot smacked the backboard, far left of the hoop. "You knew my mom?" he said.

"Yeah," Hunter said. "When my oldest sister was playing JV basketball, she never stopped talking about her. Your mom was a senior and headed for college ball. But she took the time to help my sister improve her game. She used to come over and shoot in our driveway."

"Really?" said Jake. "I had no idea."

Hunter tossed the ball back to Jake. "Let me ask *you* something," he said. "What do you think about when you're on the line during a game?"

"I don't know," Jake said. "Nothing really."

"I doubt that," Hunter said. "Be honest."

Jake sighed and tucked the ball under his arm. "I think about the crowd. How they're watching me and expecting me to miss. Then I try to think about what my mom would have coached me to do. But when I think about her, I remember she's gone and I'm . . ."

"Alone," Hunter said. "Got it. So what do you think about when you catch a pass and fire up a 3-pointer?"

"Nothing," Jake said. "I just shoot it."

"I get it," Hunter said. "When my band put together our first album, I couldn't wait to record it. We had so much fun practicing the songs until we had them perfected."

Jake smiled. He couldn't believe Hunter was in his driveway much less telling him cool stories.

"When we stepped into the studio," Hunter continued, "we had to do some parts separately. When it came time for me to sing along with the track, I could barely do it. Do you know that it took me twenty-four takes to finally get it right?"

"Really?" Jake said. He shot another free throw and made it.

"Yep," Hunter said. "You know, I was also a Tiger when I was your age. When I wasn't playing ball, I was watching games. I remember going with my sister to one of your mom's games once. She played great but got called for a travel in the fourth quarter. Her team lost, and she blamed herself."

"Huh," Jake said. "I've never heard anyone say anything about that."

"She felt pretty bad about it," Hunter said. "We wanted to say hello after the game, but we didn't even dare. She looked inconsolable."

"What's that mean?" Jake said.

"Like, you can't be helped," said Hunter. "Like, no person or words or cure can help."

"That's how I felt when she died," said Jake.

"I believe it," said Hunter. "When I heard about it myself, I was really sad. I'm sorry, Jake."

Jake didn't know what to say.

Hunter dribbled the ball a few times. He said, "So how about this. Instead of trying to get out of your head when you're at the line, why not just focus on someone else?"

"Like my teammates?" Jake said. "Or Coach Davis or something?"

"Why don't you give your dad a chance?" Hunter said. "Instead of thinking about how alone you are, think about your dad sitting in stands watching you. He thinks you're going to make that shot every time. Besides, your mom being gone is tough on him, too. You guys are a team." He passed the ball to Jake.

Jake smiled and shot another free throw. *Swish.* "How about a quick game of horse?"

"I won't let you win," Hunter said. He grabbed the ball and dribbled out near the 3-point line and put up a shot. It looked on target but bounced off the rim. "But then again, I may be a little rusty."

Jake and Hunter played H-O-R-S-E. If Hunter was rusty, it didn't show. It was a close game, but Hunter squeaked out the win. Jake didn't mind. He was actually having fun playing basketball again.

"Thanks for the game," Hunter said. "I need to take off. Big concert tomorrow night, you know. I have a lot of prep to do."

"Thanks for hanging out," Jake said. "My friends aren't going to believe we played horse."

Hunter smiled. "Make sure to tell 'em who won."

CHAPTER 9

TOURNAMENT TIME

Saturday morning was a blur. Jake woke up, showered, and gobbled up his breakfast. It was tournament day, and he couldn't wait to take the court. As he was eating, he kept thinking to himself, *was Hunter Moon really shooting H-O-R-S-E in my driveway last night?*

Jake's dad drove him to the gym and dropped him off by the locker room. "Good luck, kid," he said. "Remember, one for luck and one to relax. Go get 'em."

"Thanks Bad," Jake said. "But remember what I said. No yelling!"

"Okay, okay," his dad said. "I may wave again, though." He winked at Jake before he left.

Once Jake and his teammates were dressed and ready for the first game, Coach Davis came into the locker room for a pregame pep talk.

"Did everyone have a good breakfast?" Coach Davis said. "You're going to need it. This is a four-team tournament, so we'll be playing two games. We play the Palmetto Prowlers first in about half an hour. I need everyone on the bench to be ready today. If some players start to get tired, I'll be subbing in and out quite a bit."

"The Grizz never gets tired," Chuck said.

The team laughed. Some even threw towels at him.

"Your mouth doesn't," Coach Davis said. He smiled and gave him a friendly wink. "Okay, here are our starters. Mike, Chuck, Leo, Reggie and . . ."

Coach Davis paused for a moment.

Jake popped up off his bench, "Jump Shot Jake is ready, Coach," he said. He looked Coach Davis square in the eye as he said it.

"Hmm," Coach Davis said, "okay. Show me what you got, JJ."

Mike grinned and nodded at Jake.

As they rushed out of the locker room, Reggie slapped Jake on the back. "What's gotten into you?" he said.

"You wouldn't believe me even if I told you," Jake replied.

"Try me," Mike said.

"I played H-O-R-S-E with Hunter Moon last night," Jake said.

"Hunter Moon?" Mike said. "*You* played hoops with *Hunter Moon* last night?"

"I told you that you wouldn't believe me," Jake said. "Apparently he knew my mom. He's pretty cool and a good shooter, too."

Soon the Tigers and Prowlers were ready for the tipoff. Jake jockeyed for position against his guy. This time, the player set to guard him was a little shorter and thinner than Jake.

The referee blew his whistle and tossed the ball up in the air. Reggie and his opponent took off like two rocket ships firing into the air. For once, Reggie did not reach the ball first. His opponent tipped the ball with two fingers to the Prowlers point guard.

The Tigers slid back on defense. Jake's man never stopped running. He was moving around screens, running back and forth. He wasn't big, but he was quick. Their point guard threw him a pass as he came around a pick. He turned and shot the ball for an easy basket. It was 2-0, Prowlers.

Reggie inbounded the ball to Mike, who brought it up the court. The Tigers set up their offense to create a wall on one side of the lane. Jake sprinted toward and around it, rubbing his man off on the screener. Mike threw a perfect chest pass to him, and Jake went up for a shot. Just as he released the ball, the Prowlers' center hacked Jake across his shooting arm. Despite the contact, Jake's shot went in.

Tweet!

"That's a foul on number thirty-three," the referee said, pointing at the Prowlers' center. "Count the basket. Shooting one."

Jake stepped to the line.

Jake tried not to think. But trying not to think made him think about last night, shooting with Hunter Moon. He began to hum "Blowin' Off Steam," just to relax.

As he started his dribbles, he heard his dad yell out from the crowd. "Come on, Jake! You've got this. No sweat!"

Jake smiled. *No sweat,* he thought. He took a deep breath and released his shot. The ball bounced high on the front of the rim.

Jake held his breath and watched the ball carom off the backboard, roll around the rim, and finally drop through the net.

The Tigers' faithful roared.

As they ran back to play defense, Chuck looked at Jake, laughing. "That was ugly," he said, "but it worked."

The rest of the game belonged to the Tigers. Jake kept getting fouled but managed to make five of his ten free throws. Not great foul shooting, but an improvement. It wasn't great, but it was better. Grizz was a monster on the boards, which helped them get a lot of second-chance shots. Leo had five steals playing against the Prowler's best scorer.

At the final horn, it was Tigers 65, Prowlers 52. They'd won the first game of the tournament. Now, they would be playing for the championship.

CHAPTER 10

BATTLING THE BEAST

The Tigers huddled by their bench for the second time that day. The Crofton Cardinals had won to meet the Tyndall Tigers in the championship game. The Cardinals were familiar foes, but not ones Jake was looking forward to facing.

"Another team, another win," Coach Davis said. "Who's going to win today?"

"Tigers! Tigers! Tigers!"

High-fives all around, and the Tigers took their spots on center court.

Jake knew who his opponent was before he even stepped foot on the court.

The Beast.

The teams positioned themselves for the tip off. Jake looked at The Beast and thought, *Has he grown even bigger since the last time we met?* Jake certainly didn't want to repeat his poor performance on the last occasion he faced the Cardinals and The Beast.

The Beast leaned in and snarled in Jake's ear. "I hear you're making some of your free throws. I don't buy it."

The ball flew in the air, and Reggie shot up to tip it to Mike. Just as Mike took off for the hoop, The Beast flung his elbow around. It caught Jake in the chest and knocked him to the floor.

A whistle stopped the game as quickly as it had begun. The referee called a non-shooting foul on The Beast. The Beast just smiled, happy with the message he'd sent: *This will be a rough game.*

Jake didn't care. "Try it again," he said. He wasn't about to back down to this kind of bullying. And he would keep in mind a tally of The Beast's fouls. He now had only four fouls left to spend.

The Tigers inbounded the ball, but Mike threw a poor pass and turned it over.

The Cardinals brought the ball up the court, and Jake stuck to The Beast on defense. They ran a play, but Jake had seen it before. It was a screen play set up to get The Beast an open shot. Jake danced around the screen and threw his hand out, deflecting the ball. It went right to Chuck who tossed it down court to Mike who was already on his way for the easy layup. Two-zip, Tigers.

The Cardinals scored on their next possession. When the Tigers got the ball back, Coach Davis called out the play. Mike held up two fingers as he dribbled up the court. This time, Jake curled off of his pick, caught the ball, and popped an easy 16-foot jumper before The Beast could catch up.

"That's the JJ we know!" Mike said as the Tigers ran back on defense.

On the low block, The Beast started to talk trash. "So, you're not afraid to shoot anymore, eh?" he hissed. "Good. I was hoping for that."

Before Jake could respond, he realized the Cardinals' point guard had beaten Mike. Jake was too late to help and watched the point guard dribble right past for an easy bucket.

Mike threw the ball to Leo on a quick outlet. Jake sprinted up court, and Leo let fly with a long pass. Jake stormed to the hoop. He went up for the layup and the next thing he knew, his shot was blocked, and he was on the floor.

Jake looked to the ref for a foul call, but there wasn't one.

"No easy ones, Bricklayer," The Beast said, standing over Jake.

The Cardinals started playing better defense on the Tigers. Mike dribbled and slashed enough to find open shooters. Leo started out four-for-four as Reggie and Chuck battled in the paint. Jake made three shots and went to the foul line three times, drawing multiple fouls on The Beast. Unfortunately, Jake missed all of his free throws. After each miss, The Beast talked trash.

As the second quarter was winding down, the Tigers had the ball. Leo threw a cross-court pass to Jake. Jake raised the ball to shoot, but The Beast was all over him. Jake pump-faked. The Beast bit on the fake, and Jake jumped into him. The boys collided, and the ref blew his whistle.

"Keep it up, Hacker," said Jake. "One more and you're on the pine."

The Beast sneered, but he now had four fouls. One more and he would foul out of the game.

Jake stepped up to the line and wiped his hands on his shorts. He thought of his mom and then his dad. He took his two dribbles. One for luck and one to relax. He fired away.

Clang!

Jake shook his head. On his second shot, he just let his mind go blank and lofted his shot. The ball caught the back of the rim, bounced around, rolled, and dropped.

Jake sighed. "No sweat," he said to himself.

At halftime it was 32-31, Cardinals.

In the locker room, Coach Davis rubbed his hands together so fast the team expected them to start smoking. "Yes!" he said. "That's how we play. These guys are tough, but you guys are taking it to them. You're operating like a well-oiled machine. A lawn mower! In the second half we need to really turn up the blades. Just like the first half, but faster. Mulch them!"

"Wait," said Chuck, "I'm confused. I thought we were ants."

His teammates all chuckled. Coach Davis sprung over the locker room bench and grabbed a fistful of Chuck's jersey, pulling Chuck in close.

"Not today, you're not, Grizz!" Coach Davis spat out. "You, you're not even a lawn mower. You're the Grizz! You're our bulldozer. I need you boxing out. I need you pushing and leaning on them so hard that they end up on their butts!"

With each sentence, Coach Davis pulled Chuck's face closer to his. Chuck winced and turned away.

"What's the matter?" Coach Davis said. "Does my breath stink?"

"Uh, yeah," Chuck said.

Coach Davis let Chuck go. He cupped his hand in front of his mouth and breathed into it. "Yikes," he said. Everyone burst into laughter.

As the Tigers prepared to take the court for the second half, Coach Davis called Jake over. He stopped chewing his mint gum long enough to say, "Cooper, you're in. Jake, take a seat."

Jake was on the bench again.

The game resumed, and Jake stared blankly at the court.

Jake grabbed a towel and put it over his head. He wondered why he was benched. He rested his chin in his hands.

Jake looked over his shoulder. He found his dad sitting in the 14th row. This time, he was sitting next to some guy wearing a sweat suit, a ball cap, sunglasses, and holding a basketball. Jake's dad looked at him and gave him a thumbs-up. The guy next to him looked at Jake, smiled, and gave the basketball a spin, letting it balance perfectly on his finger.

Jake tried not to laugh out loud. Hunter's outfit was even more ridiculous than last time. As Jake turned his attention back to the game, he remembered that he was still stuck on the bench while he teammates took the court.

"Hey," Coach Davis said, "chin up. This isn't what you think. It's been a long day, and I just want you to get a little rest. That guy's playing you hard out there. When the fourth quarter comes, you're going to out there and run circles around him, okay?"

"Okay," said Jake.

Coach Davis pulled the towel off Jake's head. "Now, drink plenty of water."

Cooper played well. Coach Davis rotated the other bench players in one by one. Only Jake sat through the entire third quarter for the Tigers. Jake looked over at the Cardinals bench. Their coach was leaning forward, watching every dribble and pass. Just behind him, The Beast was reclining on the bench. He looked back at Jake and started cracking his knuckles. Jake got the message.

Before the quarter began, Jake walked over to Mike. He said, "Keep an eye on me, Wizard. I'm feeling good." He wasn't about to let The Beast intimidate him.

Mike grinned. "You've got it, JJ," he said.

The game was a battle. The Cardinals were strong inside and continued to score despite the best efforts of Reggie and Chuck. Mike held up his end of the bargain and kept flinging the ball to Jake, who put up quick shots and dribbled around would-be defenders. His shot was on fire. The Beast struggled to guard him without fouling him.

Late in the quarter, Reggie ripped down a rebound and tossed the ball to Jake in the corner. Jake set his feet for the shot, but caught The Beast coming from the corner of his eye. He looked like he had every intention of using that last foul.

Jake pump-faked, and with a quick dribble, dodged to the side. The Beast flew by him, slashing at his wrists, but missing. Jake fired up the shot for a 3-pointer.

With a mere ten seconds left on the clock, the Cardinals had the edge, 62-60.

The Tigers brought the ball up the court. Mike drove the lane and kicked it out to Leo in the corner with a chest pass. Leo launched an 18-foot attempt, but the ball hit the rim and bounced straight up.

Reggie leapt up for the rebound. As he grabbed for the ball, a defender slapped at it, sending it flying right to Jake on the wing.

Jake heard the crowd counting down with the clock — *three, two, one.* He let his jump shot fly just as The Beast crashed into him.

Jake was on the floor when he heard the whistle over the crowd's roar.

"Count it," yelled the referee. "Plus one."

Jake had tied the game, but now he had to go back to the line again.

Time had run out, so there was no need for rebounders. It was just Jake at the free throw line, all alone.

As The Beast walked off the court, he bumped into Jake. "How many free throws have you made this game?" he said. "Oh, that's right. One lucky shot. And how many have you missed? Let me get my calculator!"

"Ignore him," Mike said. "You're the man."

Jake rubbed the sweat from his hands on his shorts. *You're not alone,* he thought to himself. *Your team is right behind you. Dad is in the stands. This is the kind of moment Mom trained you for.*

Jake dribbled two times. He paused with the ball at his waist and took one deep breath. He brought the ball up and muttered, "No sweat."

As soon as Jake released his shot, he knew it was too strong. The ball soared up past the rim and hit the backboard. But then it went in. He'd banked it in!

Jake threw his hands on his head as his teammates rushed the court to congratulate him.

The Tigers had won the tournament.

CHAPTER 11

BLOWIN' OFF STEAM

After the game, the Tigers were celebrating in the locker room. No one was in a rush to get home. Reggie turned on his portable speaker and grabbed his phone. In seconds, the first few chords of "Blowin' Off Steam." They all pumped their fists in the air as the music reverberated around the locker room. When Hunter's voice came through the speaker, they all bellowed along. They were the tourney champs, and it was time to celebrate.

Coach Davis, who'd been in his office for a moment after the game talking to the hometown reporter, walked into the room.

Jake's dad was right behind him. He walked over to Jake and gave him a big hug.

"Dad," Jake said. "I'm all sweaty."

"Who cares?" his dad said. "You did it!"

Suddenly, the music stopped. Coach Davis was standing next to Reggie, holding his phone.

When the music stopped, the whole team stopped singing along, but they could still hear it. It was like the music stopped, but Hunter's voice was still loud and clear. Coach Davis grinned and extended one hand toward the locker room door. The door swung open, and Hunter Moon walked in, still singing.

The team was even more quiet than before. Hunter stopped walking and then stopped singing. He walked right over to Jake. "Nice job, kid," he said. "Your mom would be proud."

"You changed clothes," Jake said. "Good call."

"What?" Hunter said. "You didn't like the sweatsuit?" He ruffled Jake's sweaty hair.

Jake grinned.

Hunter spun on his heel to face the team. "I hear there's a concert in town tonight. Who wants to go?"

Like the reveal of a magic trick, Hunter reached into his pocket and pulled out a handful of tickets, fanning them out for the team to see.

The guys went nuts. It took a half an hour before Chuck stopped singing, Mike stopped dancing, and Jake stopped smiling.

Later that day Coach Davis drove Jake's dad and the whole Tiger team to the Hunter Moon show on the team bus. Once inside, Jake's dad walked over to Jake and his friends. "Can I borrow my son for a bit?" he said.

"Yes, sir," Chuck said.

"Jake, let's go grab a soda," Jake's dad said.

The pair walked toward the concessions. "That was a heck of a game you played today," Jake's dad said. "Your mom would have been proud of you. I'm proud of you."

"Thanks," Jake said. He noticed that they'd walked right past the concession stands. "Where are we going? The soda is back there."

"We need to do a quick stop first," Jake's dad said. He walked up to a man in a hat that said "Security" and showed him a piece of paper.

"Go on in," the security guard said.

"What's going on?" Jake asked.

"Nothing much," said his dad. "Hunter just wanted to congratulate you."

"Really?" Jake said. "Cool."

As they were talking, Jake heard the drums on stage begin to thump rhythmically. Then a guitar began to play. It was "Blowin' Off Steam."

"Dad! I don't want to miss this one!" Jake said. He looked through the crowd to where his teammates were going wild.

Suddenly Hunter Moon was standing above Jake on the steps to the stage. "Come on, buddy," he said. "We have a show to start."

The guitars continued to play the same riff over and over in a loop. The spotlight popped on, and there was Jake standing alongside Hunter Moon in front of thousands of fans in their hometown.

"Hey there, Tyndall!" Hunter yelled into the microphone. The crowd roared back. "Who here saw that basketball tournament today?"

The crowd yelled some more.

"Then you know who this guy is," Hunter said. "This, my friends, is Jump Shot Jake! Let's go!"

With that, the band blasted off. Hunter Moon, the former Tyndall Tiger ballplayer and current country music star, played "Blowin' Off Steam."

If Jake would have thought about how many people were watching him up on that stage, he might have gotten nervous. But he was too busy dancing alongside Hunter and singing his heart out.

No sweat.

ABOUT THE AUTHOR

Tyler Omoth grew up in the small town of Spring Grove, Minnesota. He has written more than forty books for young readers as well as a few award-winning short stories. Tyler loves watching sports, particularly baseball, and getting outside for fun in the sunshine. He lives in sunny Brandon, Florida, with his wife Mary and feisty cat, Josie.

GLOSSARY

airball (AHYR-bahl)—an unsuccessful free throw attempt that doesn't even hit the rim

arc (ahrk)—a curve or a part of a curve; in basketball often describes the trajectory of a shot

conditioning (kuhn -DISH-uhn-ing)—exercising to improve health and stamina

criticism (KRIT-uh-sizz-um)—expression of disapproval based on perceived faults or mistakes

gimme (gih-ME)—something very easy to perform where success is assumed

inconsolable (in-kuhn-SOHL-ah-buhl)—not able to be comforted

paint (paynt)—the rectangular portion of a basketball court from the baseline under the basket extending to the free throw line; players line up around it during free throws

stifle (STYE-fuhl)—to stop or to hold back

taunt (tawnt)—to tease or try to make someone mad

DISCUSSION QUESTIONS

1. Basketball is a team sport, yet Jake felt very alone when he was shooting free throws. Can you think of times when players in other team sports might feel alone?

2. Jake took out some of his anger on his dad after a bad game. He was mad that his dad didn't come to many of his games, but he was also upset with himself and stressed about dealing with the loss of his mom. How could Jake have handled this situation better?

3. Sometimes team sports can lead to unsportsmanlike behavior. Who in Free Throw Fail did you see behaving poorly on the court. Did Jake ever act unsportsmanlike? What should he have done instead?

WRITING PROMPTS

1. Jake's mother was a great basketball player in her own right. Write a scene where she and Jake play one-on-one.

2. The Tigers choose many nicknames at the story's beginning. Make a list of nicknames for you and your friends or family.

3. Hunter Moon's hit song is called "Blowin' Off Steam." Write the lyrics for the song.

MORE ABOUT
FREE THROWS

The worst free throw shooter in the NBA might have been Chris Dudley. Dudley, a center who played for five different teams from 1988–2003, averaged a mere 45.8 percent from the charity stripe over his career. He once went 0-13 from the line in a game in 1990.

The great Wilt Chamberlain has missed more free throws (5,805) than anyone else in NBA history. For his career, he made just 51 percent. But he had hot streaks, and in his record-setting 100-point game, he made 28 of 32 free throws.

The average success rate on free throws in the NBA is about 75 percent. In college basketball, 69 percent is the average.

The most free throws shot in one pro game was 39 by Dwight Howard in 2012. Howard, who played center for the Orlando Magic in that game, made just 21 of the 39 free throws. However, Howard finished with 45 points and 23 rebounds and his team won the game, 117-109, over the Golden State Warriors.

The record for most consecutive free throws made in practice is 5,221. Ted St. Martin set the record in 1996 at age 59, and the record performance took him more than seven hours to complete. St. Martin grew up on a dairy farm in Yakima, Washington, and was a backup guard on his high school team.